Bears Barge In

Written by Joni Sensel
Illustrated by Christopher L. Bivins

First Edition

dreamfactory

Dream Factory Books
Enumclaw, Washington
www.DreamFactoryBooks.com

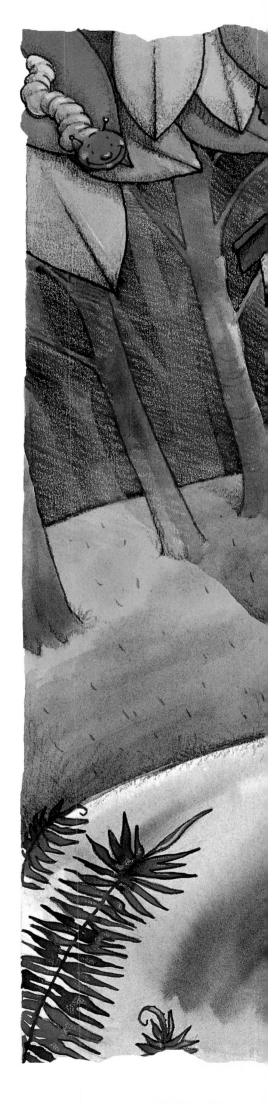

Once there was a house
in the woods.

Inside the house lived one
clever child…

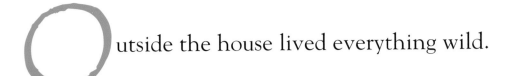utside the house lived everything wild.

There were crickets and cougars and badgers and bears,
opossums and owls and herons and hares.

They were friends of the boy. Zack was his name.
Unlike the animals, Zack was quite tame.

They all thought the woods were a great place to play. In fact, visitors sometimes decided to stay.

And as much as Zack enjoyed chatting with squirrels,

he'd rather play with boys and girls.

So...

5

Once there was a house in the woods.
Soon there were two. Then two became four.

And then there were more
and more
and
more. . .

'Til houses stretched from door to door.

The woods had filled with toys and tools and barbeques and swimming pools.

All that remained was a wee grove of trees.
Beneath them, the animals all tried to squeeze.

Throats growled. Eyes flashed.
Hair bristled. Teeth gnashed.

They jostled there for room to live…

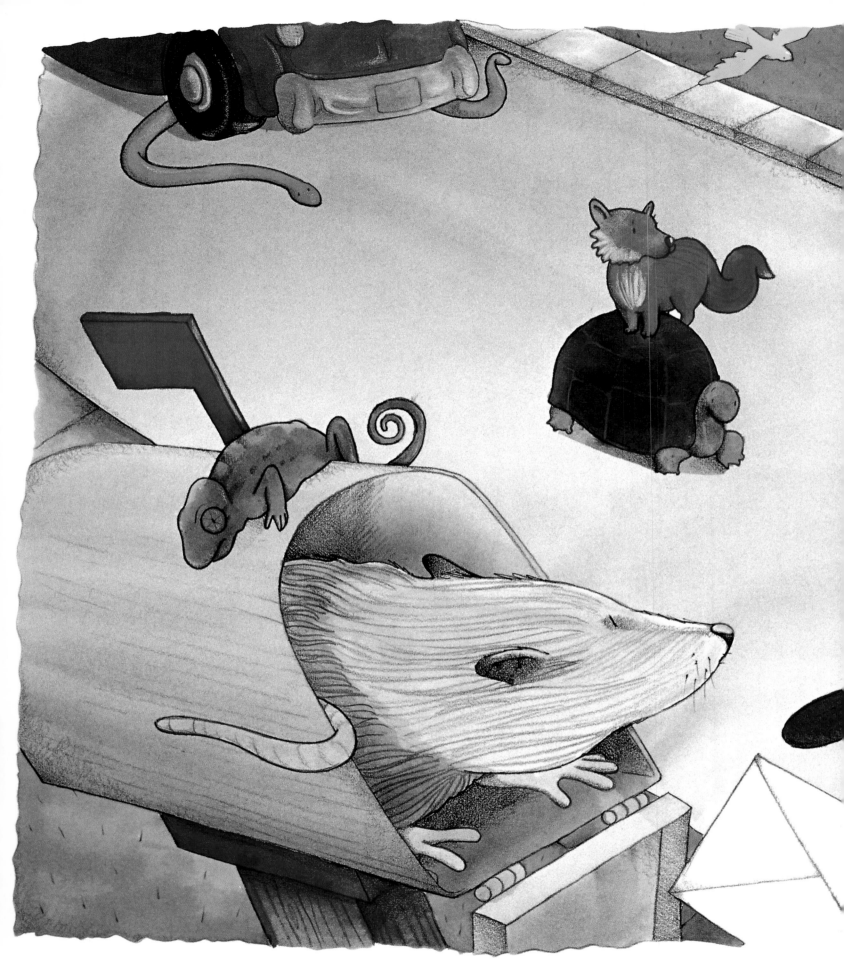

$\mathcal{U}$ntil something finally had to give.

One night the critters overflowed
and started prowling down the road.

13

W

hen Zack woke up, to his surprise,
a 'possum swung before his eyes.

He tiptoed out without a sound.
Can you imagine what he found?

Chipmunks in the cupboards,
woodpeckers on each wall,
raccoons in the refrigerator,
hornets in the hall.

16

Coyotes curled in closets
while snakes swarmed up the stairs.
And the bathroom? There was no mistake.
The tub was full of bears.

Zack's neighbors simply flipped their lids.
"No bears allowed! They'll eat our kids!
They'll eat our poodles for a snack!
We're sure to have a bear attack!"

Zack answered, "Just because they're hairy
doesn't mean they're bad or scary."

Despite his words the neighbors growled,
"No animals with fangs allowed."

They built a huge fence all around,
from the highest roof to the lowest ground.
Their houses they picked up with cranes
and yanked in tight with hooks and chains.

They put up signs and posted guards
and hung out locks with access cards.

When it was done they gave a shout:
"There! That will keep those critters out."

The neighbors firmly closed the gate.
Zack stayed outside to watch and wait.

Time passed. Vines grew.
Rain dripped. Leaves blew.

No bears ate Zack. Zack ate no bears.
He lived his life, and they lived theirs.

And now that there was room anew,
the animals found new homes, too.

Zack's bathtub had cleared out by spring
('though one bear left a dreadful ring).

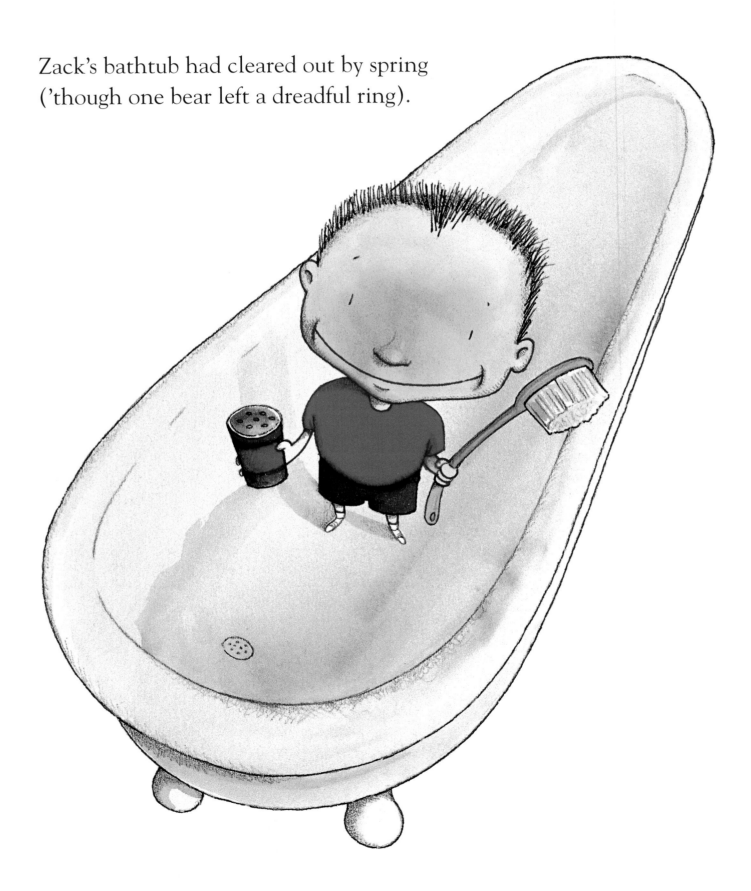

Once the neighbors all had proof
no teeth had chased Zack up his roof,
the other kids came back to play —
If Zack could dodge bears, so could they!

Sometimes their footprints on the trails
crossed prints from hooves or paws or tails.
Zack often heard faint howls at night
or saw wild eyes reflecting light.

Such sightings made Zack's neighbors fear
and shout to him, "Come hide in here
where you'll be safe!"

"No thanks," Zack said.
"I'd rather stay out here instead."

Tips from Zack and his friends
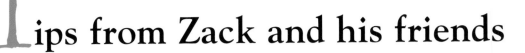

If you live near wild animals, you can help all of your neighbors — people and animals — get along. Here's how:

- Be smart, be aware of what's around you, and remove temptations that might get animals in trouble.

- Keep trash in a can with a snug lid, and put the can in the garage or shed before dark. Don't leave it out for hungry noses to find.

- When your family has a barbeque, volunteer to clean the grill afterward so food odors don't attract unwanted guests.

- Feed pets indoors and store their extra food inside, too. At night, put them indoors or in a kennel with a roof to keep them safe.

- Bears love birdseed too, so bring bird feeders in at night and take them down for a few weeks if you suspect a bear may be visiting.

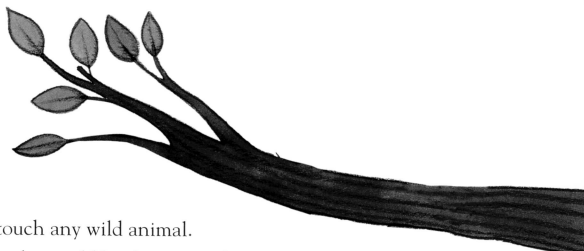

● Don't feed or try to touch any wild animal.
It's not good for them and it could be dangerous for you.
Enjoy watching them from a distance.

● Stay near home in the very early morning and
around sunset, since that's when you're most likely to bump
into roaming bears and cougars.

● Most wild animals will hide if they see (or smell) you before you
see them. If you're lucky enough to spot a wild animal, stop where
you are. Don't yell, but make noise by clapping your hands or
whistling loudly. Stay near friends or grown-ups. Raise your arms
or coat so you look big. If you're scared, back away slowly. The
animal almost always will sneak away the first chance it gets.

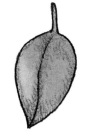

Most animals that visit
simply need a little space.
We all can be good neighbors
if we leave them a wild place.

A portion of the proceeds from this book will be donated
to The Nature Conservancy, which helps to make sure
animals have homes and space of their own.

Thanks to Scott Smith for inspiration; to
U.S. West, Donnie Martorello, and Kevin
Bacher for encouragement and support; and
to the students of Ms. Rebecca Crews' 1999/
2000 first-grade class at Kibler Elementary in
Enumclaw for their help and advice!

Dream Factory Books
P.O. Box 874
Enumclaw, Washington, 98022, USA
www.DreamFactoryBooks.com
877-377-7030

Printed in Canada
5 4 3 2 1

Sensel, Joni, 1962-
      Bears barge in / written by Joni Sensel ;
    illustrated by Christopher L. Bivins. -- 1st ed.
      p. cm.
      LCCN: 00-191001
      ISBN: 0-9701195-0-X

      1. Animals--Habitations--Juvenile fiction.
    2. Human-animal relationships--Juvenile fiction.
    3. Animals and civilization--Juvenile fiction.
    4. Stories in rhyme.   I. Bivins, Christopher, 1961-
    ill. II. Title.

    PZ8.3.S467Bea 2000   [E]
                    QBI00-562

Parents — contact the publisher for a free parents'
and teachers' guide supporting this book.